Talking Story with Nona Beamer

Stories of a Hawaiian Family
by
Winona Desha Beamer

Illustrations by
Marilyn Kahalewai

The Bess Press
P.O. Box 22388
Honolulu, HI 96823

Editors: Ann Rayson and
Marilyn Kahalewai
Cover Design: Marilyn Kahalewai
Typesetting: Stats and Graphics

Library of Congress Cataloging in Publication Data
CATALOG CARD NO.: 83-70357
    Beamer, Nona
    Talking Story with Nona Beamer: Stories of a Hawaiian Family
    Illustrated by Marilyn Kahalewai
    Honolulu, Hawaii: Bess Press
    80 pages

ii

TABLE OF CONTENTS

PREFACE

These Hawaiian stories grew up with me:

"some are old - some new -
some legend - some true."

I treasure family tales - told, sung and danced - and with each generation a little special magic was added. My sons, *Keola* and *Kapono* Beamer, have written lovely music that endear these stories even more to today's *Hawai'i*.

I have told and sung them in classrooms across the State of *Hawai'i*, across our nation and abroad.

The joy of storytelling is worldwide, and telling Hawaiian stories has a special excitement because of the *aloha Hawai'i* enjoys throughout the world.

Personal joy is transmitted more lovingly when a story teller is inspired by the warm faces of listeners. Now that I am a grandmother, I take great delight in telling these stories to my grandson *Kamanamaikalani* Beamer. His response to these stories is very creative and has added new sounds and motions to my stories.

As you read these stories I can see your faces and feel your aloha.

Mahalo (thank you) for joining us in love.

Me ke aloha,

Nona Beamer

A LEI FOR KEOLA

It was a beautiful Hawaiian beach day. I loved watching my two sons playing in the sand. My heart overflowed with love as I admired their fine healthy bodies and listened to their voices as they played happily together . . .

AT THE TIME of our story, *Keola* was six years old. We were sitting on the beach near *Punaluʻu* on the Windward coast of *Oʻahu*. It was warm and sunny and the beautiful *Koʻolau* Mountains were floating in lazy white clouds. *Keola* and his younger brother, *Kapono*, were bringing small shells and pieces of coral to me, as they dug in the sand.

Suddenly, I noticed that *Keola* was very quiet. He was looking all around him. First, his eyes would be on the mountains, then along the curve of the shoreline. He left his brother and came to sit beside me, as though he had a special secret to share with me.

1

We were sitting on the beach near Punaluʻu, on the Windward coast of Oʻahu.

"Mommie, wasn't the dear Lord kind to us?"

"Yes, *Keola*, the dear Lord has always been very kind to us all, but why do you ask?"

"Because, Mommie, I think he was extra kind to us."

And again, his little head turned this way and that as he looked at the land, the sky, and the sea.

"Everything beautiful that the dear Lord made, he put a *lei* around. He put clouds around the mountains. He put the shade around the trees, and the waves around the islands. Wasn't he kind to give all those beautiful things a *lei* to wear?"

That was a very wonderful thought, coming from the heart of a six-year-old Hawaiian boy. What a precious gift *Keola* gave us, a lovely part of his heart that we can pass on to our friends.

With each telling, the warmth of his heart is extended further and further.

"A *Lei* for *Keola*" is so beautiful that I thought it should be told in a poetic Hawaiian chant:

HE LEI KEAKEA
The White Lei

He lei keakea noho mai la i ka mauna
> The soft white lei encircles the crest of the mountain

Ka mauna ki'eki'e i luna kū kilakila
> The mountain high above standing in great majesty

Kilakila nō luna
> Majestic on high,

Nō luna i ke ao
> Bedded in the clouds.

3

Ke ao ua malu nā kumu laʻau
        The clouds cast a shadow on the trees

Laʻau hoʻohuʻohu
        The trees so haughty;

ʻOhuʻohu hoʻohiehie
        so haughty and proud.

Hoʻohiehie launa ʻole!
        this is splendor beyond compare!

ʻAʻokle lua naʻe ke ʻike aku
        There is no beauty to equal this sight

He ʻike aku nā moku ʻo Hawaiʻi
        The sight of the islands of Hawaii

Hawaiʻi ke kuini ʻo ka Pākipika
        Hawaiʻi, the Queen of the Pacific.

Ka Pākipika ua laʻi i ka lā
        The Pacific lies calm in the sun

Ka lā hoʻolewa i ka nalu
        The sun, movingg on the waves

Ka nalu kohu lei ana
        The waves bedeck, as a lei

Lei ana i ke aloha
        A lei of love,

Pumehana me ke aloha
        Warm is this love,

Aloha e!
        It is love, indeed!

THE SLEEPY SHELLS OF PUNA

INTRODUCTION

THE BEAMER *PUNALU'U* house on *Hawai'i* was a large, sprawling white frame with a *lānai* (porch) completely around the front and sides. Low dark volcanic rock walls squared off the yard. I remember the cozy feeling of that house and the old well and bucket out back.

It was a quaint village, *Punalu'u,* and we didn't have many playmates because very few families lived there, maybe five or six within easy walking distance.

I remember grandfather, still in his sleep robe, sitting on the front steps, tending a neighbor boy's sore foot. I didn't really know his gentle ways - he was always brusque with me. But with children in pain, he was a very gentle, soft-speaking man.

The village gathering place was the spring. Women came to wash their clothes on the rocks and to talk about the *honu* (turtle) legends, about how the mother turtles would come to the spring to lay their eggs. The women would chant the turtle songs imitating, to my childish delight, the animal movements. I would happily imitate them, and giggle - giggle - giggle! The turtles had left years ago, but the older women still remembered. There were pigs now at the spring and children chasing them - and more happy laughter.

That is the scene of this family story I call the "Sleepy Shells of *Puna.*"

I have two grown sons and a small grandson who have learned to sing of the sleepy shells. Hundreds of school children and grown-ups in *Hawai'i* love to sing and dance this song.

5

THE SLEEPY SHELLS OF PUNA

There is a beautiful black sand beach on the Island of *Hawai'i*, the largest of the Hawaiian Islands. This is a very special and famous beach. The sand is black because many, many years ago, the volcano erupted and poured red hot lava down the slopes of the mountains and into the sea. When the hot lava met the cool ocean waves, great clouds of steam rose and the cool water, touching the hot lava, turned it into tiny sand-like bits of black crystal that glisten in the sun. These beautiful jewels cover the beach for miles and miles. This is the famous Black Sand Beach at *Puna*, where our story takes place.

As children, we loved to spend our summer vacations with Grandma, Helen *Kapuailohia* Desha Beamer, in her big white house near the black sands of *Puna*. There were many grandchildren in our family. I had three brothers, a sister and thirteen cousins. We all loved the black sand beach and we especially loved our Grandma. We called her "Sweetheart Grandma" because, to us, she was truly a sweetheart.

All the Beamer grandchildren came to spend this particular summer with Grandma. We were everywhere - outside, climbing the old lava walls, dropping stones into the well, and chasing the pigs along the only road in Puna.

In the middle of this road, there was a pond filled by a gurgling freshwater spring. It was the custom of the village women to meet here everyday and wash their clothes in this pool. It was, also, the delight of the Beamer children to play and splash about in this little pond. This was not always appreciated by the plump and busy Hawaiian women.

One day, after we had played all the games we knew and explored all the nearby caves, we wanted to be in the house with Sweetheart Grandma. This happened to be

It was the custom of the village women to meet here everyday and wash their clothes in this pool.

"You children go down to the beach and see if each of you can find a pair of shiny shells."

one of her busy days. She was cleaning the big house and doing the cooking for her large family.

We sat and watched her for awhile. Soon we were trying to help her with the cleaning and cooking. But, instead of helping her sweep, we were only making a lot of dust. And, instead of helping with the cooking, we were dripping *poi* all over her kitchen floor. Finally, with a sigh, she set her broom aside and gathered us around her. With a twinkle in her eye, she said:

"My *mo'opuna* (grandchildren), I know you are all trying to help me and that makes me very happy. Now that you have finished all the hard work, there is very little left for me to do. Why don't you run down to the beach and play?"

Sweetheart Grandma could see that we didn't like this suggestion. There wasn't a single smiling face among us. We all wanted to be with her that day.

Seeing that we were not happy, she drew us closer to her *mu'umu'u* (Hawaiian dress) and said:

"Why don't we make up a new game? You children go down to the beach and see if each of you can find a pair of shiny shells. They should be two shells of the same size, shape and color."

This was an inviting game, but not an easy one. There are many, many shells on the sandy beaches of *Hawai'i*, but not many are the same size, shape and color. But because we wanted to please Sweetheart Grandma, we all scampered down the beach. We searched for a long time and didn't return to the house until the sky was aflame with a beautiful Hawaiian sunset.

Not all of us had found two shells alike, but we held up our prizes for Grandma to see and admire. After she had exclaimed happily over our treasures, she asked us to sit in a circle around her. While we were looking for our shells, Sweetheart Grandma had been busy writing a new song for us:

9

PŪPŪ HINUHINU

Shiny shell

Pūpū hinuhinu, pūpū hinuhinu e
Shiny shell, shiny shell

O ke kahakai, kahakai e
I found you by the sea,

Pūpū hinuhinu e.
Shiny shell.

Pūpū hinuhinu, pūpū hinuhinu e
Shiny shell, shiny shell

E lohe kākou e
I hear the sound of the ocean,

Pūpū hinuhinu e
Shiny shell.

Pūpū hinuhinu, pūpū hinuhinu e
Shiny shell, shiny shell

E moe, e moe, e moe, e
To sleep, now to sleep, to sleep.

Sweetheart Grandma was very wise. Not only did we stay out of doors so she could finish her housework, but we fell in love with the song of the shiny shells. We asked her to teach it to us so that we might sing and dance it in a Hawaiian hula. And always, after we had put the shells to sleep, we would place them on the floor, curl up beside them and fall fast asleep.

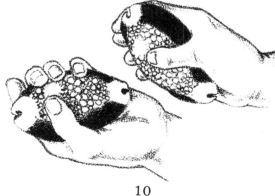

KA HANA KAMALI'I IN KONA

HOW OFTEN HAVE Hawaiian mothers asked the question: *"Auwē, ka hana kamali'i?"* (Oh dear, what are the children doing?) How often have we watched, puzzled at the antics of the youngsters?

The Hawaiian *keiki* (child) has a secret language, like all other children of the world. It is not that we, as adults, do not acknowledge and appreciate this secret language. It's just that the adult world has perhaps lost sight of the simple imagery so vivid to the imaginative and uncomplicated mind of a child.

Sweetheart Grandma (Helen *Kapuailohia* Desha Beamer) had an unusual gift for sharing this special children's world with us - not only in story, song and dance; but she actually recreated the scenes, scents and colors of our world.

On this particular day, everything was especially beautiful. How warm the sun felt! The breeze was mild and gentle, and the sand felt good between our toes. It was a fine *Kona* day, and we stretched our legs until our feet tickled. Many children were on the beach - noisy, happy Hawaiian children. It was a wonderful day for splashing, and the waters of *Kailua* Bay were very inviting. It was a good day for boats to bob around, too.

Suddenly, from around the point, came a funny looking ship. It was high on either end and low in the middle, with many poles sticking up in the air. This was the cattle ship *"Humu'ula,"* which was named for a place on the slopes of *Mauna Kea* (white mountain), on the Big Island of *Hawai'i*.

As the ship came closer, we could see many large animals crowded together on the low deck. We could even hear the loud animal noises. I suppose they were tired after their long trip. I know I would have been tired if I had been pushed together like those animals, and had come from *Kaleponi* (California) on that funny boat.

The men on the ship began grabbing the animals around their necks and tying blindfolds over their eyes. It looked as if they were playing a game, but the blindfolds worked like magic and soon the animals were quiet. They stopped making those loud "mooing" sounds, and stopped tossing their big horns from side to side.

We watched carefully as the men on the ship took hold of long lines hanging from the high poles. They tied these lines under the *opu* (stomachs) of the cattle and lowered them slowly into the water.

There were small rowboats waiting alongside the ship. The *paniolo* (cowboys) tied the horns of the animals to the gunnels of the rowboats, unfastened the long line that went swinging back to the ship, and the rowboats set off to the shore.

The *paniolo* rowed hard, and we could see their bulging back muscles as they pulled the oars and sang in loud, deep voices:

"'Uhene la, 'uhene la, 'uhene la, 'uhene"

("Hooray tra la, hooray tra la, hooray tra la, hooray")

As the rowboats neared the shallow waters, the men untied the blindfolds and hit the *pipi* (cows) on their broad *'okole* (backsides). The animals quickly swam to shore.

Can you imagine how surprised the fish were? They began to wiggle and splash! Some of them even jumped right out of the water! The fish had never seen such strange animals with long horns swimming in the ocean beside them! They seemed to be very excited.

We were excited too! We watched as these great slow-moving animals came out of the surf. They looked like huge rocks - if rocks could move around. Some of the children on the beach were frightened and began to

huddle close together, but I wasn't frightened; I was just curious! We wanted to get close enough to touch the animals, but *"Auwē!"* ("Oh dear!"), they smelled so bad we had to hold our noses and keep our distance!

The *paniolo* were on their horses ready to lead these strange animals through the village of *Kailua-Kona*. They were then herded up the road to the hillside where they could eat fresh, green grass and rest.

What an exciting day this was! We all began to talk at once, while we jumped up and down and "mooed" just like the animals. We tied our shirts and towels over our eyes and bumped into each other. We put our fingers to the sides of our heads and pretended that we had long horns. We were so noisy that we made more noise than all of the animals put together. What fun it was! When I stopped to catch my breath, I could laugh harder than any of the other children.

Suddenly, we noticed that a crowd of adults had gathered around us. They were all shaking their heads, and some were frowning in a very puzzled manner. They were saying:

"Auwē!! Ka hana kamaliʻi?"

(Oh dear, what are these rascal children doing?")

We were telling the story of the cattle coming to *Hawaiʻi*.

13

We tied our shirts and towels over our eyes . . . put our fingers to the sides of our heads and pretended that we had long horns.

When the sun began to set we started home. Grandma was laughing with us as we all walked along the road. She began to sing a happy song and as we listened closely, we heard:

Ka hana kamaliʻi
> What are the children doing?

ʻUhene la, ʻuhene la, ʻuhene la, ʻuhene
> Hooray tra la, hooray tra la, hooray tra la, hooray.

Hōʻole ʻuʻula
> There is no denying

ʻUhene la, ʻuhene la, ʻuhene la, ʻuhene
> Hooray tra la, hooray tra la, hooray tra la, hooray.

Kamano iʻa ula
> (Imitating) the red fish

ʻUhene la, ʻuhene la, ʻuhene la, ʻuhene
> Hooray tra la, hooray tra la, hooray tra la, hooray.

Pipi wai aʻo Kaleponi
> (Imitating) the cattle from California

ʻUhene la, ʻuhene la, ʻuhene la, ʻuhene
> Hooray tra la, hooray tra la, hooray tra la, hooray.

Kawele ia mai
> Tying on the blindfold

ʻUhene la, ʻuhene la, ʻuhene la, ʻuhene
> Hooray tra la, hooray tra la, hooray tra la, hooray.

Paʻa ka ʻōnohi
> Tightly over the eyes

'Uhene la, 'uhene la, 'uhene la, 'uhene
> Hooray tra la, hooray tra la, hooray tra la,
> hooray.

Ha'ina mai ka puana
> Tell the refrain

'Uhene la, 'uhene la, 'uhene la, 'uhene
> Hooray tra la, hooray tra la, hooray tra la,
> hooray.

Ka hana kamali'i,
> What are the children doing?

'Uhene la, 'uhene la, 'uhene la, 'uhene
> Hooray tra la, hooray tra la, hooray tra la,
> hooray.

To this day, when I can't sleep at night, I don't count
sheep jumping over the fence; I count cattle leaping out
of the surf!

Historical note: The first cattle landed in *Hawai'i* on February 14,
1793. This was during Captain Vancouver's second visit here. Captain Cleveland landed the first horses at *Kawaihae, Hawai'i,* on May
24, 1803.

THE PROMISE OF
THE TREE SHELLS

IN THE BEAUTIFUL forests of *Hawai'i* there live tiny shells called *kāhuli*. They were so named because of the curious way they turn from side to side when they walk. They live in the cool branches of the *hau* trees and on the leaves of the *kī* (ti) leaf plants. They are beautiful little animals, snails of delicate pink, yellow and green.

Our story begins a long, long time ago, before *Hawai'i* was discovered by the sea captains of Europe. Legends tell us that these tiny shells inhabited the Hawaiian forests by the millions. It was the habit of the little shells to crawl down from their tree-top homes to search along the mountain streams for a lovely fern called the *'ākōlea,* with beautiful bright red blossoms. The blossom was filled with sweet nectar, and they would eat and eat until their tiny shell stomachs were full. Then they would climb back up into the trees and fall fast asleep.

A day came when the animals of the forests looked out over the ocean and saw sailing ships approaching the islands. They began chattering in a most excited manner because they had never seen such a sight. The ships landed on the sandy shores of *Hawai'i*, and the creatures of the forest were stirred from their afternoon naps by the sound of loud, heavy footsteps entering their quiet land. What a frightening experience for all the living things of the woods! Cows, horses, and other large animals were coming to live in the Hawaiian forests.

At first, the little tree shells were too frightened to move or even make a sound. But soon their stomachs were so empty that they knew they must go once again to the stream beds to search for the bright red *'ākōlea* blossoms. But, alas, they feared that if they left the trees and walked along the forest floor, many of them would be

17

trampled under the hooves of the large animals. In great concern, they held a council meeting of their elders high in the leafy tree-tops. The other animals of the forest could hear them saying:

"What shall we do? What shall we do? We are so hungry. We have not tasted the sweet nectar of the *'ākōlea* for many days. What shall we do?"

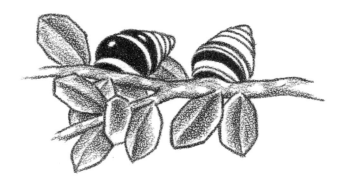

Their friends the birds were sitting in the tree branches and they listened to these sad words. They were the *kōlea* birds, who had shared many happy and carefree days with the tree shells. The birds cocked their feathered heads and thought about the sad little shells.

"Little shells, little shells," said the *kōlea*, "we are your friends, and we will help you. We will fly down to the streams where the *'ākōlea* blossoms grow, and bring the sweet nectar to you." When the little shells heard this they were very excited and happy. "Oh yes, oh yes, our friends, the *kōlea* birds will help us. We will no longer be hungry."

Just then, a very old and very wise tree shell began to shake his head.

"Now, now. Before we ask the birds to do this for us, let us think of something we can do for them."

So, once again, all the little tree shells were silent as they thought and thought about doing a favor for the *kōlea* birds. Then, suddenly, the birds and the shells heard a small squeaky voice coming from under a young *kī* (ti) leaf plant. As the voice grew louder and clearer, they were amazed to find that it came from the tiniest of all the tree shells.

"Listen, listen, everyone," said the tiny shell with the big voice. "We can do something very wonderful for our friends, the birds. We can promise to sing to them every night of the full moon."

This pleased the *kōlea* birds very much. They loved to hear the sweet trilling notes of the tree shells as their singing filled the forest air.

"It is agreed," said the birds. "We will fly down to the streams where the red *'akōlea* grows and fill our beaks with sweet nectar. Then we will fly back to the trees and feed you until you are no longer hungry. In return, you will sing to us every night of the full moon."

When the *'akōlea* blossoms heard this, they were very happy. They, too, were friends of the tree shells. They put their pretty little heads together and whispered in low tones,

"Let us put on our brightest red dresses. It will be easier for the birds to find us among the green leaves."

When the birds flew down to the streams, they found many beautiful bright red *'akōlea* blossoms. After they had sipped the nectar, they flew swiftly to the *kāhuli* shells. It wasn't long before the *kāhuli* shells, full of nectar, fell happily asleep.

Since that day long, long ago, the tree shells and the *kōlea* birds have kept their promise. Every night of the full moon, the forests of *Hawai'i* vibrate with the high trilling notes of all the tree shells singing to their friends the *kōlea* birds.

This is the song they sing:	And this is the story they tell:
"Kāhuli aku	"Turn little tree shell
Kāhuli mai	Turn back again.
Kāhuli lei 'ula	Here is a red lei
Lei 'akōlea	The lei of *'akōlea.*
kōlea kōlea	Little bird, little bird
Ki'i ka wai	Go down to the stream,
Wai 'akōlea	Bring the sweet nectar of
Wai 'akōlea"	The *'akōlea."*

When I taught this song to my grandson *Kamana,* he put his teeth together and made a "Zzzzz" sound after the song. The sound reminded me of the trilling notes of the *kāhuli,* so now we all sing it with a "Zzzzz" and it's a happy sound.

"The kōlea birds will help us."

THE GOLDEN LEHUA TREE

INTRODUCTION

MOTHER WAS *ONO* (hungry for) sweet mountain watercress.

"Sure" said brother Towhead. We saddled our horses and meaded *mauka* (toward the mountains) above the reservoir of *Kamuela* town.

I loved my horse *Kahua*. He was a Lord Brighton thoroughbred, stood 18 hands high, and was single gaited! What a joy it was to ride him, like sitting in a comfy easy chair, the hoofs all hitting. It made me sit tall in the saddle and survey the town nestled in the green crazy patterned landscape below. It was an exhilarating gallop to the top, riding easy up the gentle slopes. Now we turned laughing, gasping, happy!

We had empty *poi* bags tied to the pommels of the saddle. They were the old fashioned cloth *poi* bags like half-size pillow cases of strong muslin. When we got to the reservoir we found the large leaf, sweet mountain watercress, sometimes tough to pull up by the roots. We filled our bags and thought how happy our dear mother would be to have so much sweet watercress. We could hear her light laughter and we spoke about it, laughing out loud. As we turned to begin the downward trot, I saw a brilliant yellow tree halfway down the slope.

"What is that tree?" I asked my handsome brother.

"That bright yellow one? A *ma-ke* (mah-kay). Die, dead tree" he replied. "You wanna see it?"

Can't be *ma-ke,* die dead tree" I said. "It's too bright and yellow."

Were we surprised when we cirrcled it and all but embraced it with wide open arms. It was a vibrant golden *lehua* tree, the *'ohi'a mamo* - the first golden *lehua* tree we

23

had ever seen! How gorgeous! I began to pick branches and lay them across the saddle until the pile came up to my chin. I would have enough to box and send to several friends. We had found the rare golden *lehua!*

Later, when my children were little, I thought it would be nice for them to hear stories with a Hawaiian background, and from this charming *Kamuela* experience I told them the story of the golden *lehua.*

THE GOLDEN LEHUA TREE OF HAWAI'I

ON THE ISLAND of *Hawai'i,* the largest island in the Hawaiian group, there are miles and miles of *lehua* trees growing in great numbers. They grow out of the lava rocks, covering the land with beautiful soft green leaves and brilliant puffs of red fluffy blossoms.

At the time of our story, the forest was aglow with *lehua* trees, all in bloom. In the midst of the forest, there was a little *lehua* tree that was very, very sad. Its limbs drooped, almost touching the ground, and its branches had very few leaves. Every night, the sad *lehua* tree could be heard sobbing and sighing: "Oh dear, I wish I were beautiful like all the other trees." And then, the little *lehua* would sob and sob until it fell asleep.

One night when the forest was very quiet and a beautiful full moon was shining brightly, the *menehune* (elves) heard the little tree crying. They looked and looked, and when they found the sad *lehua* tree they formed a circle around it and asked, "Little *lehua* tree of the woods, what makes you so unhappy?" The tiny tree answered, "I wish I were as beautiful as the other *lehua* trees in the forest."

Then it cried and cried until it fell asleep.

When they found the sad lehua tree they formed a circle around it.

The *menehune* disappeared into the forest to think about the unhappy tree and, when they saw that the little tree had fallen fast asleep, they silently tiptoed back and joined hands in a circle around it. They bowed their heads and said a very special blessing for the tree. As soon as they had finished the blessing, they quickly scampered away to hide behind the rocks and other trees.

When dawn came into the sky, all the trees began to awaken and whisper excitedly to one another. They were saying, "Oh, look everyone! Will you look at the little *lehua!!*"

The noise awakened the sad *lehua* tree. It rustled its branches and, to its great surprise, it found itself covered with beautiful green leaves and the most glorious *lehua* blossoms. But its were not red blossoms like those of the other trees; they were beautiful golden blossoms.

"Oh dear," said the little tree, "Will you look at me! Am I not the most beautiful *lehua* tree in all of *Hawai'i?*"

The *menehune* were hiding behind nearby rocks and, when they saw the happy little tree, they just couldn't be quiet any longer. The forest was filled with the tinkling sound of their joyous laughter.

"Oh," said the *lehua* tree.

"That sounded like the laughter of the *menehune.*" Then it looked down at the soft earth near its roots and saw many tiny footprints. "Oh my," it cried with happiness.

"The menehune were. I can see their footprints. They have given me a special blessing. I am truly the happiest *lehua* tree in all *Hawai'i!*"

That is why to this day, the Golden *lehua* tree is the most beautiful *lehua* tree in the forests of *Hawai'i*, for it was given an everlasting blessing by the Hawaiian *menehune.*

26

HAʻINA-KOLO OF WAIPIʻO

THERE IS A lot of legendary, historic and romantic material left to the scholar today concerning the secluded valley of *Waipiʻo*. An aura of enchantment, of mysticism, has surrounded that beautiful spot since 1415 when the *Puʻuhonua*, or place of refuge *"Pakaʻalana,"* was built.

Long before *Kiha*, father of King *Liloa*, the goddess *Hiʻiaka*, youngest sister of *Pele*, fought a bitter battle at the mouth of the valley with *Makaʻu-kiu,* the evil shark god.

From *Kapuo-a* where the trail climbs upward to the head of the valley in the region of the mist, to *Mahikiwae-na* where dwelled the *Mahiki*, fierce *moʻo* (lizards) who had strange physical powers to leap and jump like giant grasshoppers, all the areas were a part of a legendary pattern.

This valley was a chosen place of the gods, where they kept watch constantly. The trails were guarded by the cliff spirits, and the garden land, lush and verdant, was kept rich and fertile by a myriad of quick flowing waterfalls fed by low hanging rain clouds. There was a still, quiet rhythm of living things. The very earth itself hummed with the vibrancy of growth and flourishing life. There was spiritual power present everywhere - amid the taro patches, the fish ponds, the banana and breadfruit groves. Even the low, handformed lava walls were strengthened by the surge of tide and winds. The scattered palms were deep rooted, seeming a timeless haven for the sea and cliff birds.

There were several small villages spread over the valley floor and clinging to the fringe of the cliff. All these families felt the awe and power of the great *mana* (spiritual strength) that hovered over *Waipiʻo* and came to rest as the living part of everyday life.

Lono was the deity of *Pakaʻalana,* a *heiau* (temple) of

There were several small villages spread over the valley floor . . .

most sacred *kapu* (taboo). There was *"Ke hale o Liloa,"* (the house of *Liloa*), where his bones were placed to rest after the good king died.

Liloa had inherited the right of royal sovereignty from *Wakea,* god of light, and the temple *Paka'alana* was famous over all the land. Since its inception, it had gained great reknown throughout *Hawai'i* for its extreme power to invoke the presence of the gods. Here was a revered *heiau*, a refuge for the noble and common man alike, a well-spring from which flowed the gifts of mind and heart. To the ill and infirm came well-being, to the seeker of knowledge came enlightenment, to the heart-sore and soul-sick came the peace of the great temple.

It was to *Waipi'o* that the woman, *Ha'ina-kolo* came. She had married a king of *Kukulu 'o Kahiki* (ancestral homeland of the Hawaiian people). For reasons known to *Ha'ina-kolo* alone, her husband had deserted her. Not being accustomed to the foreign land of her husband's birth, she longed deeply for her own *Hawai'i*. Finally unable to dislodge the deep longing for her home, she swam back to *Hawai'i*.

Arriving at *Waipi'o* in a state of famine and exhaustion, she hastily appeased her hunger by eating eagerly of the *'ulei* berries. It was a practicing custom to first acknowledge the gods and to make a humble offering of prayer and substance. In her state of distress, she had neglected to perform this necessary ritual of humility. Having consumed a quantity of berries, she was immediately beset by extreme weariness of mind and body. Collapsing under a clump of brush, she fell into a deep sleep and, during her state of enforced slumber, *Keoloewa,* the demon god, took possession of her mind.

Because the gods of *Waipi'o* were offended, *Ha'ina-kolo* was to remain afflicted to wander the vast wilderness, distraught and neglected.

After much time had passed, her husband, realizing

his love for her, sought her whereabouts and his search brought him to *Waipi'o*. He was told of the mad woman of the forest.

"Her hair is matted about her face, her eyes look without seeing, she utters strange sounds and will run if you approach her."

The saddened husband was in despair. Could this creature be his wife?

Suddenly the skies were darkened by a watery downpour, *Kaiāulu*, the violent rain squall that arises with fierce urgency from the uplands of *Waimea*. This was interpreted as a good omen and, encouraged by this sign, the husband set out for the forest. He did glimpse a strange, thin woman, but only at a distance. He heard her quiet mournful chant, the tones barely audible. He saw her sitting, her body void of spirit, swaying to and fro with the wind that blew the tall clumps of *pili* grass. Yes, the woman was *Ha'ina-kolo* and the *ho'āe'āe* (love) chant he heard her utter was one of love that he knew well - for had not she chanted it to him many times during their courtship? He ventured closer to the pathetic figure of his wife and began reciting with her. The days of their early love came back to him clearly. He detected a slight stiffening of her frail body as he continued to chant, approaching her slowly as though bringing a frightened animal out of hiding. Her face was a mask of curious expressions. Her mouth formed words he could not hear; her hands trembled noticeably as she attempted vainly to smooth her fern-matted hair. Suddenly, tears of joy and recognition streamed down her weathered face. It was a long and tender embrace, followed by another and yet another as she stared unbelievingly at her husband.

Before *Ha'ina-kolo* could be cured of her affliction, prayers and offerings would have to be made at *Paka'alana* to appease the gods and to ask forgiveness. She was to fashion a *kī* leaf bundle of *'ūlei* berries, climb the *pali*

He saw her sitting, her body void of spirit . . .

(cliff) unaided and gain entrance to the outer wall of refuge.

Due to her weakened condition caused by exposure to the extreme elements of *Hāmākua* and the lack of food, her journey to the temple was an arduous one. Her thin unprotected hands bleeding from the cliff rocks and overhanging vines, she made her way slowly and painfully up the winding trail. Her husband followed close behind her and added words of faith and love when she stumbled on the path. By the time she reached the temple walls, her fast-ebbing strength had completely disappeared. She could only gasp and plead that the gods would spare her further pain. Her stalwart husband, longing to give her his physical strength, could only add his words of prayer and encouragement. After *Ha'ina-kolo* finally managed to place her offering of berries over the *paepae* (doorsill), always looked upon with special superstition, an amazing transformation took place. She was given renewed strength and the haze that had beclouded her mind suddenly lifted. Falling to her knees in grateful supplication, she wept with great joy.

Ha'ina-kolo was united with her husband and the reunion was indeed a happy one. All of *Waipi'o* Valley shared their joy.

The temple of *Paka'alana* was destroyed by King *Kaeokulani* of *Kaua'i* in 1790 while he was waging a war with *Kamehameha.* The quiet ruins alone bear witness to that fateful day long ago.

As the years continue to come and pass, many stories of *Waipi'o* will be told and retold to each succeeding generation and students of *Hawai'iana* will continue to delight in the account of *Ha'ina-kolo* of *Waipi'o.*

Thunder rolled, lightning flashed. The gods had given the sign.

NAUPAKA, THE HALF FLOWER OF HAWAI'I

THERE WAS ONCE a beautiful Hawaiian princess. Her name was *Naupaka*. She lived on a lovely coral island in the Pacific Ocean. Everyone loved the princess because she was just as kind as she was beautiful. People came from miles around to hear her sweet, soft voice and to see her beautiful smile. She always seemed to be very happy; but one day the villagers noticed that she was not smiling.

"What is the matter?", they whispered to each other. "Why is the princess *Naupaka* looking so sad?"

Words reached the king and queen. They hurried to the princess and found her sitting by a mountain pool. Indeed, the face reflected in the water was a very sad face.

"My child," said the King, "what makes you so sad? Why has the smile left your face?"

Her parents listened quietly as *Naupaka* told of a handsome young man, *Kaui*, with whom she had fallen deeply in love. He was not only handsome of face and stature; he had a beautiful, kind, and loving heart. Above all his virtues, the princess cherished his gentle heart the most.

"Is this the young man of whom you speak, a man of noble birth?" asked the Queen. *Naupaka* shook her head. "No, he is not," she answered.

The social order of *Hawai'i*, in those days, did not allow members of the royal family to marry those of lower rank. *Naupaka* knew that this was the law of the land. The King gently put his arm around his lovely daughter.

"My child, because we love you so dearly, we wish only for your happiness. We shall consult the wise elders of the kingdom. Perhaps they will know what we should do."

35

Days passed; the elders met in council. They could offer no solution for the princess. Their advice was that *Naupaka* and her loved one should journey to a faraway *heiau*. There they would kneel at the entrance to the temple, and, in the shadows of the high lava walls, they would chant their story of love to the high priest.

For many days the two lovers journeyed over mountains and through forests. Each night at setting sun, *Kaui* would prepare a comfortable resting place of soft ferns where *Naupaka* would sleep.

Finally, travel weary but hopeful of heart, the young couple arrived at the temple. The priest listened kindly, shook his head very sadly, and in low gentle tones spoke to the couple kneeling at his feet.

"My children, it does not lie within my power to grant you your wish. It is a matter for the Hawaiian gods to decide." After praying quietly with the lovers, the venerable old man turned and slowly walked back into the temple.

Naupaka and *Kaui*, with their hands clasped tightly together, waited silently with their heads bowed. The sky began to darken and a wind rose through the trees. Suddenly, there was a torrent of rain, a loud clap of thunder and a flash of lightening. The lovers rose and, looking sadly into each other's eyes, embraced. The gods had given the sign. They had been told that they were not to marry.

Naupaka took the white blossom from her hair, tore it in half, and put the half flower in *Kaui's* hand.

"I shall go to the mountains to live my life alone; you return to the seashore. Never again will we meet."

To this day, the *Naupaka* flowers bloom in halves. When the mountain variety and the seashore variety are placed together, they form a perfect flower.

Who knows, but that someday the flowers will again bloom in whole, perfectly shaped blossoms and that the young lovers may be together in the Hawaiian heaven.

Today, when the beautiful song of *Naupaka* is sung, many of us are remembering this romantic story.

*Ka'ahumanu, favorite wife
of the great king.*

WHEN THE GODS BURNED

WHEN *KAMEHAMEHA I* DIED at *Ahu'ena Kamakahonu* in the village of *Kailua-Kona* in the year 1819, a great upheaval beset the Hawaiian people. *Ka'ahumanu,* favorite wife of the great king, set about to break the old *kapu* (taboo), thus making way for new religious ideas. She had already succeeded in converting *Hewahewa* to her way of thinking. *Hewahewa* was the highest priest of the land. If he favored abolishing the old gods, the people would unhesitatingly follow.

After Queen *Ka'ahumanu* succeeded in breaking the eating *kapu*, the *'ai kapu*, there was a period of rejoicing. Husband and wife sat together, eating of all foods; there were no restrictions. This was a new joy, though entered upon with deep pangs of conscience. The people accepted this change as a part of the new life *Ka'ahumanu* was advocating, but, in their hearts, was the deep-rooted fear of the Hawaiian gods.

High Chief *Kekuaokalani* firmly believed in the Hawaiian gods. King *Kamehameha* had trusted him to care for the sacred War god, *Kū kā'ilimoku*. The king knew that high chief *Kekuaokalani* was a good man, as firm in his convictions of love and humility as he was sturdy of muscle and bone. The days of tension brought much grief to *Kekuaokalani* and his beloved wife, *Manono,* Princess of *Kuamo'o*. Because he believed in the old ways of *Hawai'i,* his heart was saddened by the changes that were taking place. The other members of the priesthood rallied around him, constantly seeking his counsel, for they were unable to understand the breaking of allegiance to the old gods.

When Queen *Ka'ahumanu* sent forth her runners to proclaim that the temples and images were to be destroyed, a death-like silence fell upon the entire village of

Kailua. It was unbelievable; openly defy the ancient gods? *'A'ole! 'A'ole!* (No! no!) The faith of the Hawaiians, handed down through the ages, had withstood many foreign intrusions. No, this was wrong; the Hawaiian gods would not allow this.

In spite of his moving pleas to the people, High Chief *Kekuaokalani* could not quiet them. Family images were taken from huts, hidden in caves and rock crevices; they were spirited to lonely mountain areas. The gods would not be destroyed.

Kekuaokalani spoke in soothing tones to his beloved wife.

"*Manono,* dearest to my heart, I must fight for the preservation of our old ways. What will our people have left, if their gods are destroyed? What will give meaning to their lives?"

Princess *Manono,* a brave and noble woman, was not afraid. If this was her husband's cause, it was also hers.

As days passed and *Kekuaokalani* saw that the new ways imposed upon the people were bringing more and more strife and hatred, he constantly urged his wife to cast aside this burden of his. In moving chant tones, he admonished her,

"Let love alone be your burden, order will follow." But *Manono,* born of rank and accustomed to the rigors of leadership, would not turn her back upon her husband's struggle.

Festering as a slow-spreading disease, the strife soon reached uncontrollable proportions. Driven by distrust and extreme mental anguish, the people soon resorted to physical violence. On the lava fields of *Kuamo'o Kona,* a bloody battle was fought.

Kekuaokalani and other high chiefs fought bravely, united in the defense of their gods. Theirs was a battle of faith, but faith alone could not withstand the musket fire of the opposition. *Kekuaokalani* fell; he rose again to one

As torches set the temples of Kailua-Kona aflame against the dark sky, Hawaiians huddled together in the uplands.

knee to fight vainly for a brief few moments, then was silent. *Manono,* always close to her husband, gently kissed him and covered him with his feather cloak. Undaunted, she picked up his spear to fight valiantly at the side of his lifeless body. When she, too, was quiet and the battle had been lost, the strange wail of many chanting voices filled the air amid the bodies of the brave dead.

"Kou aloha la ea; kou aloha la ea; ai - e ei - e - e e e." The admonition of *Kekuaokalani* rang clear, just as he had taught them. "Your love, your love will make all things right."

As torches set the temples of *Kailua-Kona* aflame against the dark sky, Hawaiians huddled together in the uplands; their only defense against fear was to chant of *Kekuaokalani* and princess *Manono.*

"Kou aloha la - kou aloha la, E mālama kou aloha," "Your love, your love, keep your love."

In the same year (1819) *Liholiho, Kamehameha II* was proclaimed successor to his father and took his place upon the Hawaiian throne. *Liholiho* set a great love for his people far above other affairs of state. He quickly pardoned all war prisoners and returned them to their rightful positions in the village. *Liholiho* was seen in the village, talking with the people and comforting them, displaying a depth of spirit and a quiet understanding for his people. It was his love that strengthened the hearts of the people and, through his concern and help, the Hawaiians were soon fused in love once again. This was the way of the gods, the old and new gods alike.

"Kou aloha, kou aloha; Your love, your love will make all things right."

This faith and belief in love is still the strength of the Hawaiian. It will be a part of his heart, always. And, in this generosity, this is the gift he gives to the world.

43

She delighted in the cool glades of Kohakohau, where the rush of mountainwater spilled over into a quiet pool.

MANOUA, MAIDEN OF MANY RAINS

IN THE MIST that hovers heavily over the grasslands, in the cloud piles that sink slowly to the base of *Mauna Kea,* in the crisp, cool air of the *Waimea* uplands, the legend of *Manoua* was born.

John P. Parker was yet to arrive on the island of *Hawai'i.* Under the protection of *Kamehameha I,* this sea captain gentleman of quiet gaze was destined to have "a great grazing farm of many thousand acres" that would become a world famous cattle ranch.

The famed missionary, Lorenzo Lyons, had not yet begun to build the many Hawaiian churches that dot the landscape from *Puakō* to *Waipi'o* Valley.

The years that were to bring the great dynasty of the *Kamehameha* kings were far ahead, and the saddened heart of Queen *Lili'uokalani* was yet to be bared to her people.

Ka Po'o O Ka Ohu (the source of the mist) was the home of *Manoua,* the water nymph of *Waimea.* She delighted in the cool glades of *Kohākohau,* where the rush of mountain water spilled over into a quiet pool. From this serene retreat her spirit rose, waned, and floated freely with the passing eons of time.

As the sturdy Hawaiians settled in *Waimea, Manoua* watched them plant the first *hāwa'ewa'e* (sprouts from sweet potato). She saw these *ulu hou* (grow again) after each harvesting, until they covered the mountainsides. *Manoua* watched the *hānai pua'a,* (pig raising) the cultivating of *pū,* or pumpkin; the planting of *uhi* (yams) of purple, pink and white along *Pu'ukawaiwai.* She saw *Kamehameha* the Great and his *ali'i 'ohana* (royal relatives) travel down from *Pōhakuloa;* and many generations later, she listened as the village elders told of the visit of *Kamehameha* to *Waimea* and of the trails he traveled.

45

Manoua was known and loved by the Hawaiians of *Waimea;* and her pool, *Kohākohau,* was the favorite gathering place for the youngsters of the village. The cool, crisp beginning of many a *Waimea* morning would find the young girl, *Ha'ale'u,* sauntering up the *Kawaihae* road, then turning up the winding way through the fields of *ki'ahiu* (wild tea) toward *La'e La'e* village. There in the quiet uplands, she would spend hours picking *maile* (fragrant vine). These were favorite hills for age-honored pastimes.

One dewy morning, *Ha'ale'u* left her warm sleeping mat very early to journey the upward road to *La'e La'e.* Word had passed in *Kamuela* that this was the day for *"kapili-kōlea".* As the name implied, it was a game of the young boys to catch the *kōlea* birds by using the *kepau* (resin) of the *pilali* tree. The boys would gather *'ōpu'opu'u* (cocoons), tie them to stones with *puka* (hole), and then smear the cocoons with the tree glue. When the hungry birds came to feast on the cocoons, to their dismay, their beaks stuck fast to the choice morsels.

The weight of the stones prevented the birds from flying away; and the eager young boys pounced out of the brush, anxious for the catch.

As the sun moved to mid-afternoon, the young men, still full of the boisterous energy of fun, sought the *kahawai* (stream) for the refreshing swim. They would race to the pond of *Kohā kohau,* always hopeful of seeing *Manoua;* for her fame as the water nymph of *Waimea* had been passed from generation to generation. Not every village of *Hawai'i* could claim the honor of being the home of a water sprite, so the people of *Waimea* were very proud of *Manoua.*

When the noisy boys came to her pool to splash and laugh, she moved to a nearby rock to sit quietly, watching and secretly delighting in their fun. She was often seen sitting on a huge stone. Sometimes, she would be busily

There in the quiet uplands she would spend hours picking maile.

combing her hair. Her hair was long, half of it red and the other half black.

This day, as *Ha'ale'u* and her friends watched the boys swimming, a tragic event occurred. *Ha'ale'u's* brother was drowned. In spite of the frantic efforts of his friends, his body was recovered too late. This was, indeed, a sad event. If the water nymph *Manoua* had been summoned from her favorite resting place, she might have saved the boy's life. In the excitement of the tragedy, *Manoua* was forgotten. How sad she was, heartbroken and desolate. There would never again be the happy sounds of the boys swimming in the pool. Down-hearted and grief-stricken, *Manoua* left *Kohākohau* Falls the day of the burial in the nearby cemetery. She was never seen again after that day when the whole village mourned.

When her absence was noticed by the villagers, leis of *maile* and *haku* (woven) *lehua* appeared on the stone where she once sat, sunning and combing her red and black hair. It became a gesture of courtesy to honor the memory of *Manoua* when passing along the *Kawaihae* road. Various *makana* (gifts of *aloha*) constantly surrounded the stone.

Many years passed and the *Kawaikainea Kaimuloa* family, who lived near the great rock, became the unofficial guardians of the *Manoua* Stone. Their garden was aglow with *melekule* (the small golden marigolds), as these were the leis that most frequently adorned *Manoua*. The immediate area around the stone became *"Ponokapu"* (sacred in righteousness).

In recent years, there appeared a white picket fence surrounding the stone. The people of the village, filled with aloha for *Manoua,* would climb over the fence and place leis upon the stone. Even when the "giant powder" was brought to shatter *Manoua* into a million fragments, the surrounding stones, including *Pōhakuloa,* the companion stone of *Manoua,* fell apart; but the stone of the lady herself remained unscathed.

The well-known trail to the stream is now only a narrow footpath, precarious and crumbling under each step. The *Kohākohau* Falls are no longer cool and inviting for swimmers. Long ago, the falls began to turn a drab brown color, as though disinterested in their beauty now that *Manoua* is no longer there. But, the firm believing Hawaiians of *Waimea* will not forsake *Manoua* because they still remember her with aloha; *Manoua,* the maiden of many rains, will always be part of the history of *Waimea.* Whether she is spoken of in a whisper of awe, or in a loud voice of pride, *Manoua* will continue to live in the hearts of the Hawaiians who believe.

Ka'iana was invited to visit Canton, China, with Captain Meares aboard a sailing ship.

KA'IANA, THE TURBULENT CHIEF

THIS IS A STORY of Chief *Ka'iana* and how he plotted to secretly prevent the High Chief *Kamehameha* from becoming King of all *Hawai'i*.

The Hawaiian chief, *Ka'iana 'Ahu'ula,* was known throughout the latter part of the eighteenth century as *"Ka'iana,* The Turbulent Chief." When I first heard the word "turbulent," I thought of angry seas and sad feelings, which is the right mood for this story.

Ka'iana caused *Kamehameha* much worry and concern, because he was always plotting against him in mysterious ways. *Ka'iana* secretly longed for the power *Kamehameha* possessed. *Ka'iana* was a handsome Hawaiian with a mass of curly black hair and fine features. His eyes were deep-set and he had a curled moustache with a small pointed beard on his chin. He held his head high and his shoulders straight and he always considered himself to be very important. He wore his feather cape tied low across his shoulders, which gave him the appearance of being very aristocratic.

There came a time when *Ka'iana* was invited to visit Canton, China, with Captain Meares aboard a sailing ship. They stayed in China for a period of three months, and during this time Captain Meares acquired two new sailing ships, which he named "Felice" and "Iphigenia." Because *Ka'iana* was so popular with the English people in Canton, they gave him many gifts. They brought him cattle, goats, turkeys, citrus trees and other food items, which were all carefully packed for the long voyage to America. America was the early name of the United States of America before the Civil War in 1861.

Ka'iana was anxious to return to *Hawai'i*, but the journey from China to America was a long one, and, unfortunately, all the livestock died long before they

51

reached *Hawai'i*. The turbulent chief was a passenger on board the "Iphigenia," which arrived off the coast of *Hawai'i,* on December 6, 1788. Captain Douglass, the skipper of the "Iphigenia," then sailed directly to *Keala-kekua* Bay on the island of *Hawai'i*. Here, the High Chief *Kamehameha,* having been notified of their arrival by runners and conch shell blowers, sailed a small fleet of double-hulled canoes to meet the "Iphigenia." The King's royal canoes were beautifully adorned with feather standards *(kāhili),* and were greeted with a seven-gun salute from the cannons of the "Iphigenia."

Ka'iana was told that much had taken place during his long absence from *Hawai'i*. His family had remained in residence on the Island of *Kaua'i,* and bad feelings had developed between them and *Ka'eokulani,* the King of *Kaua'i*. *Ka'iana* knew this was not a safe place for his family to live. He knew he would have to think about bringing them to the island of *Hawai'i*.

Kamehameha offered Chief *Ka'iana* a position as Commander of his Army and *Ka'iana* readily accepted. On December 29, 1788, *Ka'iana* left the "Iphigenia." He had with him a very impressive array of tools, firearms and other goods which made him a very wealthy man in the eyes of the Hawaiians at *Kealakekua*.

Shortly after this, *Ka'iana* was able to arrange with Captain Douglass to sail to the island of *Kaua'i,* the oldest and northernmost of the Hawaiian islands. *Ka'iana* asked Captain Douglass to bring his family to the Big Island and the Captain agreed. Then, *Ka'iana* persuaded Captain Douglass to present King *Kamehameha* with a swivel cannon, which was immediately mounted on one of the High Chief's double hulled canoes along with some ammunition and muskets.

Because *Hawai'i* was a frequent port of call for sailing ships, the chiefs and the people were all busily engaged in trade with the many foreign visitors who passed through each year. It is thought that *Kamehameha* and his chiefs received a considerable portion of their wealth from these lucrative trading years. The two most frequented harbors at this time were those of *Waimea, Kaua'i,* and *Kealakekua, Hawai'i.* So, for a period of about four years, the islands of *Hawai'i* remained at peace.

When Captain Douglass next returned to *Kealakekua* in July, 1789, enroute to China, the principal chiefs of *Kamehameha* plotted to kill him and his crew. Their well planned scheme was disrupted when *Kamehameha,* always alert to maneuvers of violence, intervened at the last hour, and saved the Captain and his crew from certain death.

Near the end of 1789, an American fur trader named Captain Simon Metcalfe visited *Hawai'i.* He was in command of the vessel "Eleanora" enroute to China. Once again, true to his sly nature, *Ka'iana* convinced several of the principal chiefs of *Kamehameha* to join him in capturing the "Eleanora," after which they would divide the "booty" among themselves.

Again, *Kamehameha* learned of this evil plan, and intercepted *Ka'iana* and the other chiefs as they attempted to board the "Eleanora." The Great Chief *Kamehameha* was humiliated by his chiefs' actions and he ordered them taken to the stockade. Knowing *Ka'iana* to be the instigator of this evil scheme, *Kamehameha* vowed to have the turbulent chief under constant surveillance.

In the year 1791, *Kamehameha* was advised by his high priest, *Hewahewa,* to build a great *heiau* in honor of his war god, *Kūkā'ilimoku.* The *heiau* of Pu'ukoholā was built at *Kawaihae, Hawai'i,* and the priest assured *Kamehameha* that the Islands of *Hawai'i* would surely come under his reign.

Then in February, 1795, *Kamehameha* landed his fleet of war canoes at *Lahaina, Maui.* He then proceeded to *Moloka'i* and remained there with his forces awaiting a proper time to sail for *O'ahu.* He consulted with many of his counselors and secret advisers, but did not summon *Ka'iana* to these meetings. This made *Ka'iana* suspect that the counselors were plotting his death.

Ka'iana told his brother, *Namaka'eha:* "I feel that the Chiefs are conspiring to kill us." "What can we do to save ourselves?" asked his brother. *Ka'iana* replied: "We face death whether we follow *Kamehameha* or others, but if I die, see that I am buried secretly."

Soon after this, *Kamehameha* moved his fleet from *Moloka'i* to *O'ahu*, in preparation for the Battle of *Nu'uanu*. This battle would be an important step in uniting all of the Hawaiian islands under the rule of *Kamehameha*.

Ka'iana and his followers had other plans. They secretly left the army of *Kamehameha* and landed on the Windward side of *O'ahu*, joining the *O'ahu* forces of King *Kalanikūpule,* who was the last remaining enemy of *Kamehameha*.

Kamehameha landed his fleet at *Wai'alae, O'ahu*. He beached his war canoes from *Wai'alae,* clear around Diamond Head Point to *Waikīkī*. Can you imagine what an impressive sight this must have been? The warriors then advanced across the plains of *O'ahu,* and met the combined forces of *Kalanikūpule* and *Ka'iana* in *Nu'uanu* Valley.

At the head of the valley, the cliffs grew steeper on each side. *Ka'iana* and his warriors took their positions near the precipice known as the *"Nu'uanu Pali."* The *O'ahu* forces began to scatter on the mountaintops as *Kamehameha* drove them up to the ridges. Some of the warriors found a safe path down to the Windward side, but many of them fell to their deaths at the foot of the *Pali*.

Ka'iana, however, stood his ground firmly, but was finally killed in 1795 at *La'imi* in *Nu'uanu*. In accordance with his brother's wishes, *Namaka'eha* took the body of *Ka'iana* to a secret burial cave, unknown to Hawaiians to this day. It is said that the footprints of *Ka'iana* remain on

The warriors met the combined forces of Kalanikupule and Kaʻiana in Nuʻuanu Valley.

the rock where he stood to the very end as he threw his last spear into the smoke of the muskets. Ironically, *Ka'iana* was killed by the very muskets that he had brought back from China so many years before.

Kamehameha went on to become the King of *Hawai'i* when King *Kaumuali'i* ceded the Island of *Kaua'i* to *Kamehameha,* thus uniting the Hawaiian Islands.

As a young child, I remember family outings where Papa would stop the car at the top of the *Pali.* There is a rock there that marks the place where *Ka'iana* died. We would all gather around the rock at the beginning of the downward trail and my father would pray.

Everything was silent, and I always felt like crying, as we prayed for our safety while driving down the side of the mountain. We would leave leis and ti-leaves at the rock honoring the site of this famous battle. Sometimes during this prayer the wind would rise, and we could imagine hearing the sounds of the battle nearby. It was a very spooky feeling for all of us.

To this day, members of the Beamer family, and most Hawaiians, say quiet prayers for the lives that were lost in the Battle of *Nu'uanu* so many years ago. The story of *Ka'iana* is an important part of the history of *Hawai'i.* The recounting of such a story serves to heighten our appreciation and aloha for our heritage and our *Hawai'i.*

'AUKELE AND THE SKY ISLANDS

IN THE ANCIENT, far Western home of the Polynesians; in the mysterious islands of *Kua-i-Helani* (far-away *Helani*) so often mentioned in the chants, there lived a very old *Mo'o*. In the legends and stories of old Hawaii, the *Mo'o* is the general class of lizards, serpents, reptiles, and dragons.

The *Mo'o* of *Kua-i-Helani* was worshipped as an ancestor goddess of many Hawaiian families, among them, the Hawaiian Chief *Iku*. Chief *Iku* had several sons, the youngest of whom was called *'Aukele-nui-a-Iku*, or *'Aukele*, The Great Son of *Iku*. *'Aukele* was a favorite of the old *Mo'o*. Because of her fondness for *'Aukele*, she taught him many age-old secrets of power.

One day, the warrior brothers of *'Aukele* decided to sail to new lands. After much persuasion, they agreed that *'Aukele* might go with them. *'Aukele* hastily sought the *Mo'o* in her pit. She gave him many magic things: a leaf that would be a source of food for anyone who touched it to his lips; an image of the great god *Lono*; and a cloak made from a piece of her *mo'o* skin that, lifted against enemies, would cause the foes to crumble to dust. *'Aukele* placed the cloak over his shoulders and put the other articles of magic in a hollow bamboo tube. Grasping the stick firmly, he hastily set off for the water's edge and the embarking canoe.

The sea voyage was a lengthy one and soon their supply of food was gone. As the brothers lay weak from hunger on the floor of the canoe, *'Aukele* touched his magic leaf to their lips and they were revived.

The supernatural powers bestowed upon him by the old *Mo'o* enabled *'Aukele* to foresee the future happenings.

"We will sight land soon," he said. "There we will

59

find a woman ruling the island. I will speak with her." The brothers were displeased.

"Is this your canoe?" they asked.

"Did you build it? Do you know its chant?"

'Aukele then became aware of his brothers' hostility. He soon learned that their purpose in journeying from their homeland was to wage war. 'Aukele tried to persuade his brothers that their purpose should be to find new lands, not to fight and to plunder; but his pleading was in vain.

As 'Aukele had predicted, they sighted an island and were soon encircled overhead by many birds. Hearing the belligerent talk of the brothers, the birds returned to the island with the news of the approaching canoe of war. The chiefess who ruled the island was angered. 'Aukele, fearful of the animosity his brothers would cause, jumped from the canoe and swam to the shore. His brothers were angry and tossed his cloak into the sea and it was cast up on the island. The ruling Chiefess, seeing the cloak, picked it up and shook the sand from it. Since she was facing the sea, the brothers and their canoe sank to the depths of the ocean.

When 'Aukele reached the shore breathless and exhausted, he crawled up on the beach, and, still holding the bamboo tube under his arm, he fell upon his cloak and was soon asleep under a *hala* tree. As he slept peacefully, unaware of impending dangers, a large dog with quivering nostrils caught the scent of the foreign man. The dog sniffed and barked, and barked and sniffed. The chiefess, hearing the commotion, sent two of her women servants to investigate. She gave them instructions to kill whomever they found.

The old *Mo'o* of *Kua-i-Helani,* while giving 'Aukele extra-sensory powers, had also instructed 'Aukele's 'aumakua, or personal guardian spirit, to keep constant watch over the young man. The 'aumakua awakened 'Aukele,

The birds, too, were charmed by the kind nature of 'Aukele.

rebuking him for being careless and inattentive and instructed 'Aukele to receive the approaching women kindly and to call them by name. With a beguiling smile on his handsome face, 'Aukele greeted the two irate women. He so charmed them, that they were soon entranced by the warmhearted stranger and returned to the chiefess to report that they had found no one. The annoyed chiefess ordered the watchdog from her presence; but when the dog resumed his loud barking, the chiefess was still suspicious. She summoned her watchful birds. Surely if anyone were on the island, the birds would soon find him.

The great and omni-present god, *Lono,* alerted 'Aukele to the coming of the birds.

"Call them each by name.", commanded *Lono.*

"This will give you power over them and they will not harm you."

The birds, too, were quickly charmed by the kind nature of 'Aukele. When the birds described the wonderful stranger to the chiefess, she could not refrain from summoning 'Aukele. To her great delight, he was as handsome and as charming as had been reported to her. She fell deeply in love with him and soon they were married.

Time passed happily for both of them; and when a son was born, there was great rejoicing. The chiefess, in her warm love for her husband, was anxious that he learn the secret forces of nature. She commanded her bird brothers to teach 'Aukele to fly; she gave him many of her treasures and taught him the ways of the land, the seas, and even the heavens.

Because of her devotion to 'Aukele, the chiefess also wished that 'Aukele might know and love her father, *Kū-wa-ha-ilo.* Summoning her bird brothers, she asked them to take 'Aukele to the far-away land of her father. 'Aukele put on his magic cape; and, tucking the bamboo stick

under his arm, journeyed in flight to be presented to the old man, *Kū-wa-ha-ilo*.

When the father saw *'Aukele* flying ahead of the flock of birds, the venerable man, fearful of harm befalling his household, called *"Kūkū-'ena"*, the lightning, and *"'Ikuwā"*, (thunder) to protect him. But, because of *'Aukele's* magic cloak, the elements were ineffectual. *Kū-wa-ha-ilo,* impressed by the strong supernatural powers of *'Aukele,* respectfully accepted him as the husband of his loved daughter. *'Aukele* returned to his wife, pleased with his journey.

One night *'Aukele* was confronted by the *'uhane* (ghosts) of his brothers. They begged and pleaded to be released from their watery grave. When *'Aukele* awoke, he was sorely disturbed, and did not eat or sleep for days. His wife was saddened to see him so distraught. Feeling a great love for him, she told him that if he found the waters of *Kane* he might restore his brothers to life. *'Aukele* ate, slept, and was soon strengthened. His wife then directed him to fly to the land of the sunrise and to take great care that he travelled there in a direct straight line. *'Aukele* set forth with the magic cape over his shoulders and the bamboo tube clutched in his hand.

Flying high in the heaven, he saw a glow of red beneath a layer of clouds. The land far below was on fire! It was the moon cooking her food. The food had a tempting aroma. *'Aukele* waited until the moon rose to eat her food; then he caught her, held her fast, and greedily ate her meal. Not having sustenance, the moon grew very thin and became a new moon.

'Aukele passed over another land, one with many new and wonderful trees and plants. There he saw a deep pit, from which flowed a gushing spring. "This must be the spring of the water of life," he said.

Close by the pit was an old man, who appeared to be the custodian of the spring. As *'Aukele* approached him,

64

he demanded to know who *'Aukele* was and who his ancestors were. *'Aukele* spoke with the old man and told of his need of the water to restore his brothers to life. The old one instructed *'Aukele* to seek the permission of the next custodian who lived beyond a nearby bamboo forest. He cautioned *'Aukele* to proceed with utmost care, lest he brush against the bamboo stalks and cause them to resound with a great clatter. This noise would summon the brother of *Pele,* who dominated the land. He would be sorely angered and do all in his power to thwart *'Aukele's* plan.

Consulting the second guardian, *'Aukele* was told to go to the bottom of the pit. There he would find a blind woman cooking bananas. "Tell her of your mission," the guardian said. "Recite your genealogy."

'Aukele found the blind woman; and when he told her of his search and chanted his genealogy, she became strangely quiet. She groped her way to a coconut tree and sat with her back resting against the sturdy trunk. She remained in this position, not speaking nor moving. *'Aukele* felt compassion for the old woman. Taking up two young coconuts in his hands, he walked quietly toward her, chanting a plea of healing. As he held the small coconuts to her eyes, tears began to flow down her wrinkled cheeks. *'Aukele,* speaking kindly, bade her stop crying and open her eyes. "It is useless," she said. "I have had unseeing eyes since my birth." "Open your eyes!" commanded *'Aukele.* "I can see! I can see you!" the old woman cried in excitement. She hastily got to her feet, embraced *'Aukele,* and instructed him to bring her the stem of the water plant.

When *'Aukele* brought the stem to her, she squeezed the water from the plant into a coconut cup, mixed it with the charcoal from her fire, and smeared the mixture on *'Aukele's* hands. "Now your hands are as dark as the hands of the brother of *Pele*. He is a strong-willed man

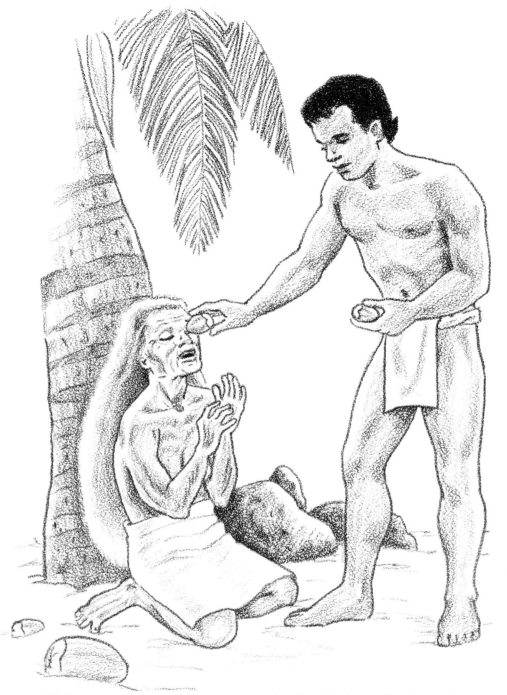

Taking up two young coconuts in his hands, he walked quietly toward her, chanting a plea of healing.

and would never permit you to take water from the spring of everlasting life." She continued, "It is his habit to frequently demand a calabash of living water from the servants of the head guardian. When night falls, and the guardian is asleep, go to the spring and hold out your hands. The servants, seeing your dark hands, will think you are the brother of *Pele* and give you a calabash of the living water."

'*Aukele* was overjoyed; at last, he was nearing the completion of his journey. Soon he would return home and his brothers would be revived.

All went well, as the old woman had predicted, but in his haste to return home, '*Aukele* brushed against the bamboo trees along the path to the outer world. Immediately, a strong wind swept through the bamboo grove; the leaves and trees surged and swayed like an angry sea. As the clamor increased to peals of heavy thunder, '*Aukele* hurried even faster to reach the rim of the outer world. Suddenly he fell to the ground, covering his ears in agony from the painful vibrations. His magic cloak fell across the calabash, preventing the precious water from spilling. He arose, shaken and confused. The bamboo tube began to move vigorously, pointing first one way, then the other. '*Aukele* hastily followed in the direction the tube pointed and found a hidden pathway, dense and overgrown. The brother of *Pele* and his warriors immediately converged upon the spot where just a moment before '*Aukele* had lain. They saw the imprint of his body in the damp earth. The broken twigs and branches gave evidence of his hasty departure. Following in an angry horde, they observed '*Aukele* flying through the heavens of the outer world. They could pursue him no further.

'*Aukele* arrived home exhausted and, with his wife, he sought the goddess of the sea and gave her the calabash of living waters. The goddess sprinkled the water over the waves, and the brothers and their canoe rose slowly from the ocean floor. There was much feasting and rejoicing as the brothers were reunited and pledged their loyalty to *'Aukele* and his chiefess. They were each given a home and lands to cultivate. There they lived, in happiness and contentment, to an age of wisdom. As time passed, the brothers' only longing was to see their parents. How happy they would be if only their parents were with them!

'Aukele agreed to bring their parents from *Kua-i-Helani*. When he arrived in *Kua-i-Helani,* the land was desolate. The people were gone, their homes rotting with decay. A dense forest had encroached from the uplands, covering the island from the mountains to the ocean. Only the old *Mo'o* remained. *'Aukele* found her near the shore, far from her *mo'o* pit. There were no traces of movement, no tracks in the sand. Her body was gnarled and grey. *'Aukele* thought she was dead. He saw that she was imbedded in the low coral reef, under a shallow depth of sand. He stamped both feet, using all the strength he could summon and succeeded in breaking the coral. He saw a movement of the old *Mo'o* body, a move that was barely perceptible. The *Mo'o* was very weak and soon would be dead. *'Aukele* remembered the kindness of the *Mo'o* and was grateful to her for giving him the knowledge of supernatural powers. He knelt in the sand, touched his magic leaf to her lips, and nourished her with food. He sat quietly at her side, stroking her rough, withered back. The *Mo'o* slowly revived and told *'Aukele* that the gods and people of *Kua-i-Helani* had gone to new homes on the islands of *O'ahu* and *Hawai'i*. She, alone, had remained to die peacefully in the old land, the land of her birth.

'Aukele returned to his home, now known as the "Hidden Island of *Kane.*" Here the god *Kane* had caused a new spring to come from the ground in order that the people of goodness might have everlasting life. Here *'Aukele* and his family live through the endless span of time,

welcoming spirits of the dead as they wander aimlessly over the skypaths in their search for the home of their ancestors. Here in the sky islands that float far above the western seas, '*Aukele* and his brothers rule as high chiefs of the '*au-makua* (the guardian spirits of the Hawaiians). Here, in the land of the perpetual glow of sunset, are the guardian gods of a proud and noble race, giving peace and haven to the departing spirits of the Hawaiian people.

As the canoes came into Hilo Bay, Kamahualele was chanting . . .

LA'A AND THE SACRED DRUM

IN THE QUIET repose of *Waipi'o* Valley, half hidden by the cliffs of *Hāmākua*, the boy *La'a* was born. His was a strange fate, a destiny created in the shadowed depths of the ancient Polynesian world.

About the year 1250 A.D. when *Mo'ikeha,* the famed chief of Tahiti, made the long journey to *Hawai'i, La'a* was but a small frolicking child. He was healthy, agile and happy. Here in the valley of his birth, he was taught, disciplined and loved by gentle *"kupuna,"* his elders.

Chief *Mo'ikeha* arrived from *Kahiki* (Tahiti) with a large company of other chiefs and their attendants. His brother, *Olopana,* and his wife, *Lu'ukia,* were his immediate family members; there were others of lesser rank and importance. The arduous voyage had been successfully accomplished through the skill and guidance of the renowned *Kamahualele,* a respected navigator, astronomer and bard. It was *Kamahualele* who sighted the green mountains of *Hawai'i* and stood on the platform of the double canoe reciting a chant to the land:

"Eia Hawai'i
E moku
E kanaka!"

As the canoes came into Hilo Bay, *Kamahualele* was chanting of *Nu'uhiva, Bolabola* and other southern islands they had passed in the course of their long, hard journey.

Later, Chief *Mo'ikeha* travelled to the mouth of *Waipi'o,* where he was honored by the friendly people of the valley. During the celebration he was fascinated by the antics of the fine, young boy *La'a.*

When Chief *Mo'ikeha* and his company returned to their Tahiti home, he prevailed upon the *kupuna* of the lad, *La'a,* to allow the boy to go with them. *La'a* would be *"keiki hānai,",* foster child of Chief *Mo'ikeha.* He would be raised as a noble son of a high chief. With the *kupuna's* consent, *La'a* became an adopted son and sailed from *Waipi'o* in the company of the great *Mo'ikeha*.

They sailed to Raiatea in the Society Islands and lived for many years in the respected, disciplined manner of high lineage Polynesian chiefs. One day there was a family quarrel, brother against brother, and *Mo'ikeha* chose to leave Raiatea, returning to *Hawai'i*. On the island of *Kaua'i*, he married *Puna's* daughter and continued to live at *Waialua*. When Chief *Puna* died, *Mo'ikeha* became King of *Kaua'i*.

The years had passed swiftly and, in his later years, *Mo'ikeha* longed to see his foster son, *La'a. Kila,* youngest son of *Mo'ikeha,* was dispatched to *Kahiki* to bring *La'a* to *Kaua'i*. With young *Kila*, King *Mo'ikeha* sent the aged *Kahuna, Kamahualele,* the skilled high priest who first brought them from *Kahiki. Kamahualele* still possessed keen knowledge of navigation and astronomy. No other had even a small portion of the vast amount of knowledge that lodged in his nimble mind.

Under *Kamahualele's* expert guidance, the fleet of double canoes departed from the southern point of *Hawai'i*. Out of sight of land, they steered by the stars and arrived safely in *Kahiki*.

The years had dealt kindly with *La'a*. He had proven himself a worthy chief. Hearing of King *Mo'ikeha's* earnest desire to see him, *La'a* assembled his large retinue. The honored prophet *Naula-a-maihea* prefaced their departure with solemn prayers, and the voyage of *La'a-mai-Kahiki* and his attendants was made in safety.

La'a had brought many gifts for his foster father, whom he had come to love. The long years of separation had served to heighten the bond of affection between *La'a* and his father, who was now an aging king. The most treasured gift *La'a* had brought from *Kahiki* was a large *pahu,* a drum covered with shark's skin. As the canoes

72

approached *Kauaʻi, Laʻa* began the rhythmic beating of the *pahu*. The people of *Kauaʻi* gathered near the shore. What was this strange, hollow, vibrating sound? Never before had such a sound as this reached their ears. Conch blasts echoed across the waters and the deep, penetrating, throbbing sounds of the drum continued to fill the stillness.

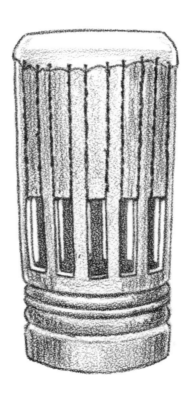

With awe and respect, people laid many gifts before *La'a*. When *La'a* was escorted in ceremonious dignity to the vast dwelling place of his father, a heart-rending reunion followed. Strong embraces, firm clasping of shoulders, and unashamed tears were exchanged by long-parted father and son. With tenderness and understanding, the wise and famed priest, *Kamahualele*, and the equally famous prophet, *Naula-a-maihea*, looked on, sharing the wonderment and joy of this warm moment. With thoughtful chants and prayers, *La'a* presented the great *pahu* to his father, King *Mo'ikeha*, who immediately decreed that the drum should occupy a place of reverence in the sacred temple and be an instrument of divine religious intent. Thus the drum was established for all time - an inseparable part of Hawaiian ritual, ceremony and religion.

When King *Mo'ikeha* died at Wailua, Kaua'i, La'a, who had established his home at *Kualoa, O'ahu*, took his three sons to *Kaua'i* to honor their grandfather, who was famed throughout all of Polynesia for his daring navigational exploits and deeds of fearless courage. These young chiefs, like their father and grandfather, were also destined to fill an honored place in their lineage. From them were descended many high chiefs of *O'ahu* and *Kaua'i*. *Kahai*, more venturesome than his other two brothers, journeyed to *Kahiki* from *Upolu* and brought hardy breadfruit trees back to *Hawai'i*. These he planted at *Kualoa, O'ahu*, dedicating anew the land of their birth. The three sons of *La'a*, grandsons of *Mo'ikeha*, honored again these islands of *Hawai'i*, so loved by their father, grandfather and by the stalwart young chiefs themselves.

And what of *La'a-mai-Kahiki*? He returned to *Kahiki*, departing from the west end of *Kaho'olawe*, which is called *Ke-ala-i-Kahiki* (the way to Tahiti), never again to point his canoe in the direction of *Hawai'i*.

When the Polynesian Voyaging canoe *Hōkūle'a* (happy star) sailed from *Hawai'i* to Tahiti in 1976, the *mana* (spiritual power) of *La'amaikahiki* sailed with them. This historic voyage proved that the young Hawaiian men of today are worthy sons of their 13th century ancestors.

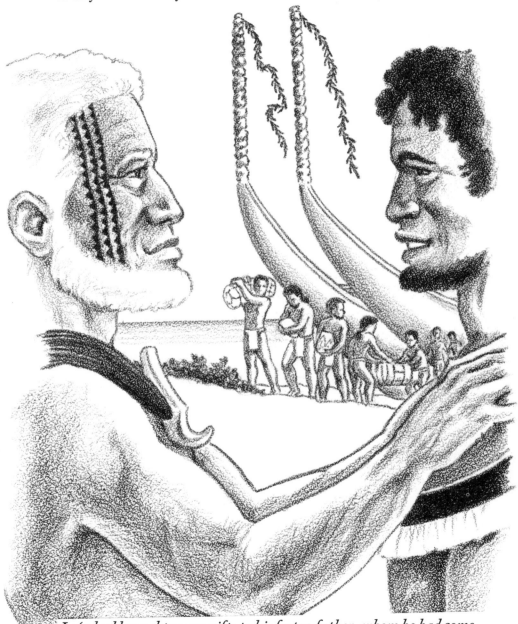

La'a had brought many gifts to his foster-father, whom he had come to love.

AFTERWORD

It is often said that "Talking Story" grew from Hawaiian oral tradition - the transmittal of culture by means of the spoken word, demonstration, chants, dance, music, and symbolic gesture. But one must hasten to add that it is more than any one of these methods of communication or even the sum of them. None can be considered talk story until it is injected with life and emotion.

Few people have developed their ability to talk story as well as the extraordinary family of Beamers. Great Grandma Isabella Kalili Desha, Sweetheart Grandma Helen Desha Beamer, Papa Francis Pono Beamer, Dambi Leiomalama Walker Beamer, Nona, and sons, Keola and Kapono, have painstakingly perpetuated this tradition with style, sophistication, and subtlety. We do not merely read their stories or hear their music or listen to them speak. We feel and share their emotions – their *aloha* for family, the *kā huli,* the *pūpū,* Honolulu's city lights, and all that makes up *Hawaiʻi.*

Nona Beamer assumed responsibility for sharing her knowledge of Hawaiiana through the talk story approach at the age of twelve while boarding at the Kamehameha Schools. She volunteered to work at the old *Kakaʻako* Mission to wash children, with "the running sores and scabs of impetigo in their arms and legs."

"I started to cry, but I knew that wouldn't help. The children looked as if they felt badly enough anyway. To calm myself, I started to chant *Kā huli Aku.* But the children's eyes grew wider and a couple of them began to cry. Without even thinking, I softened the chant by one-third of a tone and the minor chant was transformed into a major key song. The expressions on the children's faces lightened. Soon I had the little ones in the tub, soothing them with the song and cleaning their sores with soap and water.

From that moment on, I knew I wanted to teach. I knew it had to be things Hawaiian. For the next four or five years, I continued as a volunteer at the mission, telling stories and teaching the dances and songs of our Hawaii Nei."

Nona Beamer continues this beautiful tradition in *Talking Story with Nona Beamer: Stories of a Hawaiian Family.* Through this book, more of *Hawaiʻi's* youth will come to appreciate this art form and will receive the same benefits and *aloha* enjoyed by those children in the *Kakaʻako* Mission many years ago.

Neil J. Hannahs, Assistant to the President,
The Kamehameha Schools.

76